This book
belongs to:

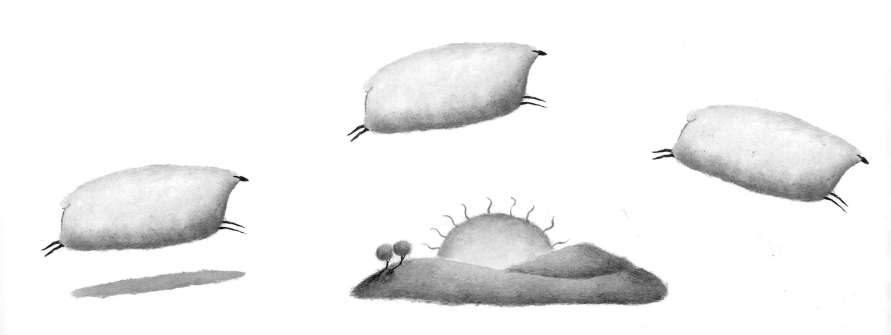

HODDER CHILDREN'S BOOKS

First published in Great Britain in 2000 by Hodder Children's Books
This edition published in 2016 by Hodder and Stoughton

4

Text copyright © Mij Kelly, 2000
Illustrations copyright © Alison Jay, 2000

A CIP catalogue record for this book
is available from the British Library.

ISBN 9781 444 91029 2

Printed in China

The paper and board used in this book are from wood from responsible sources.

FSC
www.fsc.org

MIX
Paper from
responsible sources
FSC® C104740

Hodder Children's Books
An imprint of
Hachette Children's Group
Part of Hodder and Stoughton
Carmelite House
50 Victoria Embankment
London EC4Y 0DZ

An Hachette UK Company
www.hachette.co.uk

www.hachettechildrens.co.uk

WILLIAM
and the
NIGHT-TRAIN

Written by

Mij Kelly

Illustrated by

Alison Jay

Hodder
Children's
Books

'All aboard!'

shouts the guard.
'All aboard
the night-train.
All aboard
the train that
goes to Tomorrow.'

Mothers and fathers, sisters and brothers, teachers and jugglers, zoo keepers, shopkeepers,

They're all sleepy-heads, all ready for bed,

writers and fighters, with babies in bundles and piglets in baskets – they all climb aboard.

all on their way to Tomorrow...

...with wide-awake
William, who wants
to get there most
of all.

The goods van is stacked with boxes and sacks,

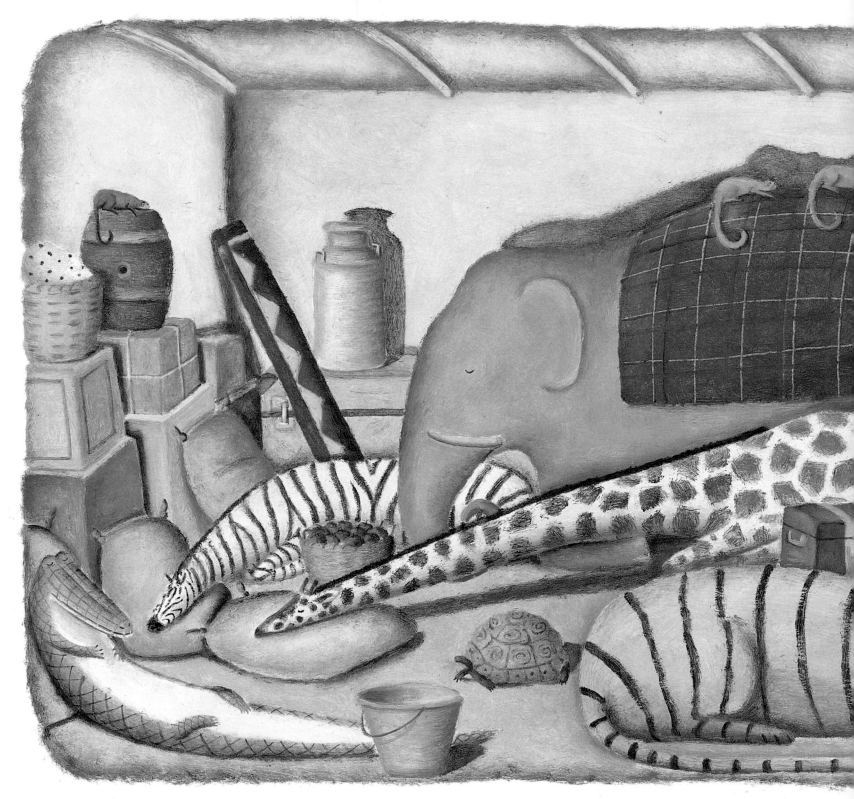

five sleepy monkeys and a huge slumbering cat.

'Everyone
sleeps on the
night-train,'
says William's
mother.
But William
squirms like
a worm.
He wriggles.
He kicks.
He wants
to get to
Tomorrow.
He wants
to get
there quick.

The guard's van is crammed
like a box of delights with balloons and kites,

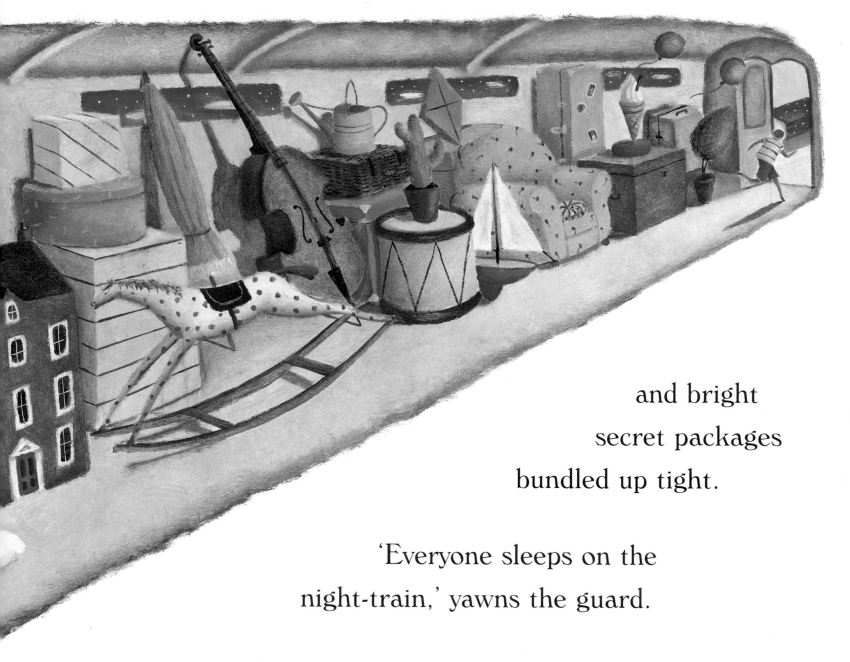

and bright
secret packages
bundled up tight.

'Everyone sleeps on the
night-train,' yawns the guard.

But William's in such a giddy rush he doesn't
want to have to hush. He doesn't care if he makes
a row. He's wide awake.
He wants to get to Tomorrow NOW.

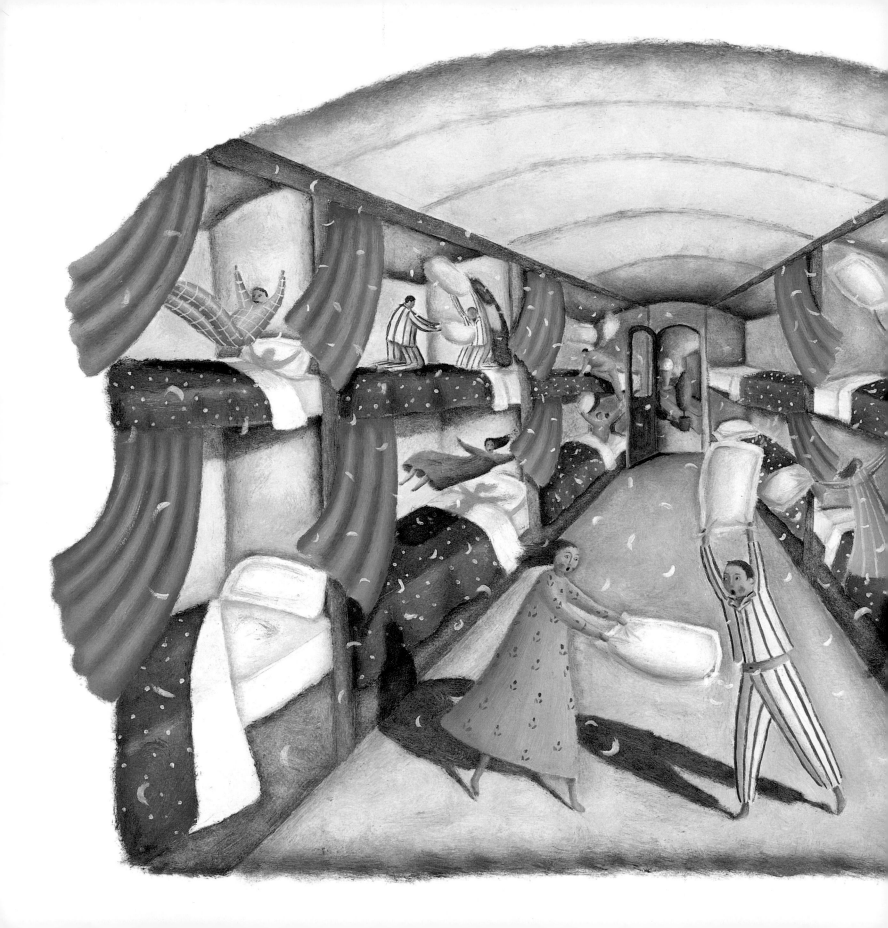

In the sleeping compartments, children bounce
on their beds and hurl feather
pillows at each other's heads.

'Everyone sleeps on the
night-train,' sighs the teacher.

But William just laughs and
charges on past. He whirls
through the feathers;
he's switched on
like a light.
He wants
to get to
Tomorrow
in the middle
of the night.

In the carriages people sit nodding in rows.
They slumber and doze. They're not wearing
pyjamas; they're still in their clothes!

'Everyone sleeps on the night-train,'
explains the writer.

But William's too busy squishing his nose.
He's too busy standing on tippity toes. He's
too wide awake. All he knows is that he can't
wait for the train to go.

'When will we get to
Tomorrow?'

Then his mother tells him about a trick that will make the night-train go lickety-split, helter-skelter, quick as a streak.

'Shut those wide-awake eyes,' she whispers.
'And shh, don't speak.'

When she cuddles him close he can hear her heart and

a soft, sudden whoosh as the night-train starts.

It pulls out of the station and into the dark,
filling the world with billows of steam,
soft see-through clouds that turn into dreams.

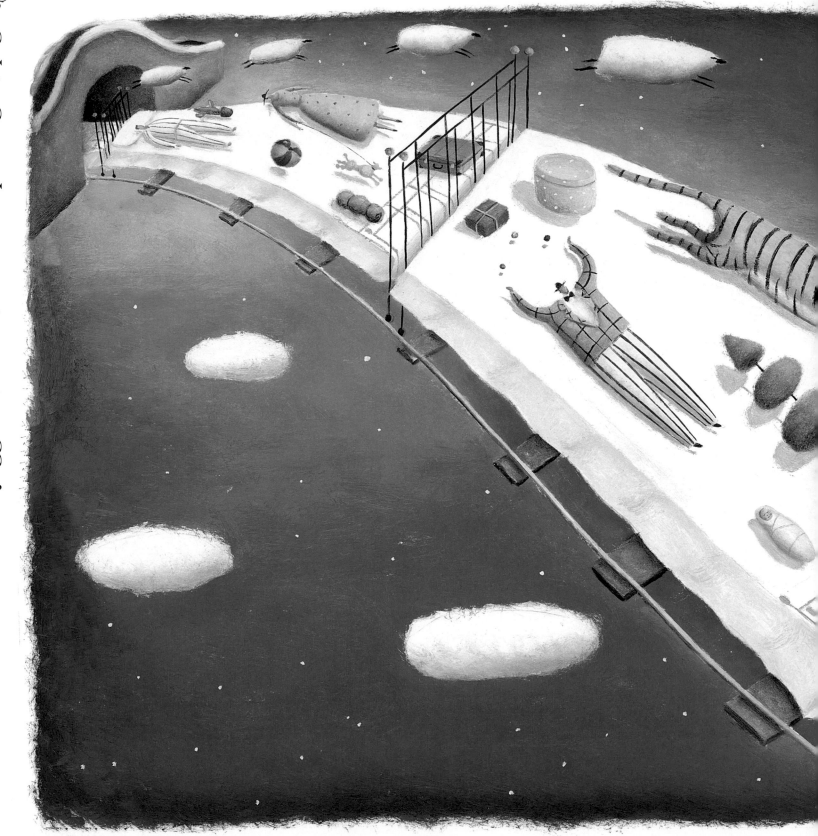

in baskets and babies in bundles, brothers and mothers and all

Teachers and jugglers, sacks, cats and packages, piglets

of the others speed out of today in the blink of an eye. Everyone *sleeps* on the night-train on the way to Tomorrow...

...even
sleepy-head
William,
who wants to
get there
most of all.

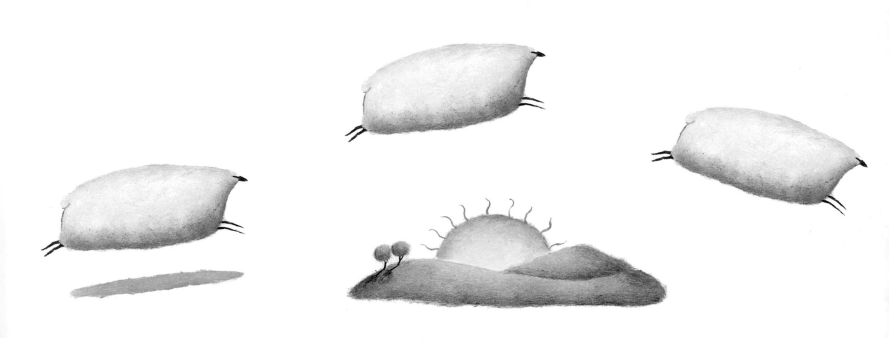

More books by Mij Kelly…

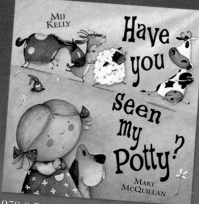

The Bump

Mij Kelly & Nicholas Allan

978 0 340 98950 0

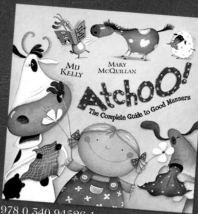

Mij Kelly   Mary McQuillan

Atchoo!
The Complete Guide to Good Manners

978 0 340 94526 1

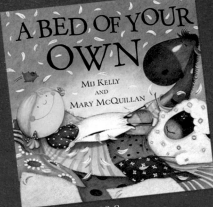

A BED OF YOUR OWN

Mij Kelly
AND
Mary McQuillan

978 0 340 99928 8

Mij Kelly

Have you seen my Potty?

Mary McQuillan

978 0 340 91153 2

One More Sheep

Mij Kelly and Russell Ayto

"…works to perfection." THE TELEGRAPH

978 1 444 91030 8

978 0 340 96000 4